KU-350-509

Tales of the Woodland

Written by
Catherine Veitch

MILES
KELLY

First published in 2021 by Miles Kelly Publishing Ltd
Harding's Barn, Bardfield End Green, Thaxted, Essex, CM6 3PX, UK

Copyright © Miles Kelly Publishing Ltd 2021

2 4 6 8 10 9 7 5 3 1

Publishing Director Belinda Gallagher
Creative Director Jo Cowan
Editorial Director Rosie Neave
Senior Editor Sarah Carpenter
Design Managers Simon Lee, Joe Jones
Senior Designer Emily Stalley
Image Manager Liberty Newton
Production Controller Jennifer Brunwin
Reprographics Stephan Davis
Assets Lorraine King

All rights reserved. No part of this publication may be reproduced, stored in a retrieval system, or transmitted by any means, electronic, mechanical, photocopying, recording or otherwise, without the prior permission of the copyright holder.

ISBN 978-1-78989-243-7

Printed in China

British Library Cataloguing-in-Publication Data
A catalogue record for this book is available from the British Library

ACKNOWLEDGEMENTS
The publishers would like to thank the following artists who have contributed to this book:
Advocate Art: Julia Seal (front cover/Blaze the Butterfly), Lucy Barnard (Diamond the Deer),
Carolina Coroa (Jasper the Jay), Annie Wilkinson (Silver the Shrew)

Made with paper from a sustainable forest

www.mileskelly.net

Blaze
the Butterfly

Illustrated by Julia Seal

One day, a caterpillar hatched from a tiny egg.
He ate lots of leaves and grew and grew. When winter
came, he hid himself away and went to sleep.

Munch!

The warm spring woke him
and he ate more leaves.

Munch!
Munch!

When summer arrived the caterpillar knew it was time to change. So he turned himself into a chrysalis, which looked just like the leaf he hung beneath. Inside, the caterpillar began to change into...

...A beautiful butterfly!

One day, when he was ready, the new butterfly emerged from the chrysalis and unfolded his wings. He was a purple emperor butterfly and his name was Blaze.

Throughout the wood there were whispers about a splendid new butterfly, and all the animals looked out for him. But Blaze was proud, and did not want to mix with the other animals.

Blaze was the talk of the wood.

"I hear he's as brave as a lion,"
said Sampson the stoat.

8

"I hear he's as purple as a plum," chirped William, a wood warbler. All the animals wanted to meet Blaze, even the bigger ones like Daisy, a gentle doe.

I hear he's as strong as a stag!

Chirp!

William, Sampson and Daisy tried to think of ways to tempt Blaze down from the trees.

"I love nibbling bark," said Daisy. So she put out some of her favourite bark, and waited.

From the treetops, Blaze could see what was happening, but he was not interested in the bark.

"Do they really think some dry bark will tempt me out of my tree?" he laughed.

Sampson did not want to give up any of his favourite food. Instead he put out some flowers that he spotted growing nearby.

"All butterflies love drinking nectar from flowers," he said.

But Sampson did not know that purple emperors were not like ordinary butterflies and did not drink nectar.

William had heard stories that purple
emperor butterflies helped to keep the
woodland floor clean by feeding on animal
droppings. But when he suggested to
his friends that they put out some
of their droppings, Daisy and
Sampson wrinkled their noses.

"I'm not doing that!" said Daisy.

"Me neither!" said Sampson.

So the animals called another
meeting to work out a new plan.

Ewww!

But William was right. Sometimes Blaze did fly down to feed on droppings. He needed the salt in them to stay healthy.

Blaze now thought he saw his chance to do just that, as Sampson and Daisy were so busy talking. But just as he landed, William spotted Blaze and hopped towards him.

17

When William had almost reached him, Blaze flew off in a flash of purple. Then William saw something amazing... there in a bush was another beautiful butterfly like Blaze, but this one was a deep chestnut brown.

The butterfly's name was Bella. William told
her about the plans to tempt Blaze, but how
no one would listen to his idea. So Bella and
William made a plan of their own.

Eventually, Sampson noticed that William
was missing, and looked around for him.

"Quick, hide!" William said to Bella.

"Who were you talking to?" asked Sampson.

Let me
explain.

Suddenly Bella fluttered
in front of everyone.

"I will help you to meet Blaze,"
she said. "But you all need to
hide while I stay here."

Flutter!

From his treetop, Blaze looked down and saw a beautiful butterfly. He had caught sight of her just before flying away from the pesky warbler. Blaze really wanted to meet her, and he forgot all about hiding from everyone.

He swooped and twirled through the air, and his purple wings shimmered in the sunlight. He spiralled lower and lower in a magnificent dance.

"Wow!" whispered the animals who were peeping through the leaves.

"Surprise!" shouted Daisy and Sampson as Blaze landed.

"You tricked me!" said Blaze. But he did not mind anymore. If Bella was friends with these animals then he could be, too. The butterflies took off, gracefully gliding up to the top of the biggest oak tree. It was a dazzling display the animals would never forget.

"Those are the most magnificent butterflies I have ever seen!" beamed William.

Diamond
the Deer

Illustrated by
Lucy Barnard

It was springtime, and many animals and plants were waking up after their long winter sleep. The wood was bursting with flowers and new shoots, and animals were busy building homes.

Diamond and Denzel were twin white-tailed deer. They were playing with an old bird's nest whilst their mother went off to graze.

Kick!

The nest shot into a tree hole. "Grrrrrrr!"

29

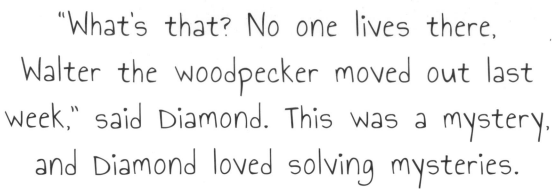

"What's that? No one lives there, Walter the woodpecker moved out last week," said Diamond. This was a mystery, and Diamond loved solving mysteries.

"Grrrrrrrr!" went the hole again.

Let's get some help!

The twins found Cruz, a hungry chipmunk, stuffing his face with nuts he had stored over winter.

"I cank awlk ow," said Cruz with his mouth full. But he followed the twins, grabbing some nuts to take with him.

Grrrr!

"Can you spit a nut into that hole?" asked Diamond. They waited as Cruz took aim... then POP POP POP! Cruz spat three nuts neatly into the hole!

"Grrrr!" went the hole.

"I told you to spit just one nut!" said Diamond.

"Uh oh!" replied Cruz, who
was talking normally now.

I hope
I get them
back.

33

"Why won't it come out?" asked Denzel.

"I'll fetch Shelby," replied Diamond. "Maybe he can help us to solve this puzzle."

34

It did not take Diamond long to find
Shelby, her friend the grey squirrel. She filled
him in on the strange sounds that had come
from the hole as they made their way back.

"Let me drop something in the hole,"
Shelby suggested.

"Ready, aim, fire!"
shouted Diamond.

Shelby threw a catkin into
the hole. They waited... but
nothing happened. Shelby was
just about to throw in another
catkin, when a strange whistle
came out of the hole.

Wheezzzzzzzz!

It was hard to hear at
first, but then it got louder,
and louder... until it was so loud
that the animals ran away.

They ran so fast that they didn't spot a turtle who had just woken up from her winter sleep. She was warming herself in the sun.

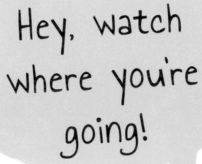

Hey, watch where you're going!

Diamond told the turtle, whose name was Tiffany, about the monster in the hole.

"Why are big animals like you scared of a whistling hole?" asked Tiffany. "I need to see this hole. Can you take me?"

39

"Look!" Diamond pointed at Tiffany.

"We can't throw Tiffany in the hole!" said Denzel.

But Diamond was pointing to the tracks on the muddy woodland floor around Tiffany.

"If we match our feet to our tracks, the tracks left over will belong to the mystery monster in the hole!"

It was a genius idea and the animals had fun finding their tracks.

The animals had worked out which tracks belonged to the mystery tree monster. But it did not help them guess its name.

So we know its tracks look like this.

"We all have different poos. Why don't we look for our poo and the odd poo out will belong to the tree monster!" said Denzel.

No one had a better idea, so the animals all looked for their poo. It was a smelly job!

EWW!

The animals worked out which poo belonged to the tree monster, but that did not help them guess its name either. They were about to give up when mother deer returned with some tasty shoots for her fawns.

Whilst tucking into them, the twins told their mother about their adventurous morning. She listened carefully and gave them an idea...

That night, the animals
stayed up to watch the hole.

After dark, something moved inside. A
catkin flew out, followed by some nuts and
lastly a bird's nest. Then a face appeared,
which looked like it was wearing a mask.
This was not a monster at all, but a
sleepy raccoon who had moved in!

The mystery was solved. All of the
animals welcomed their new neighbour.
Although Tiffany stayed hidden, because
raccoons sometimes eat turtles!

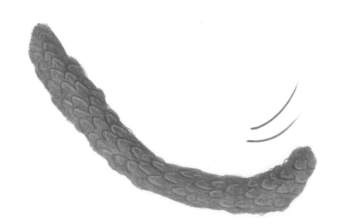

Jasper the Jay

Illustrated by Carolina Coroa

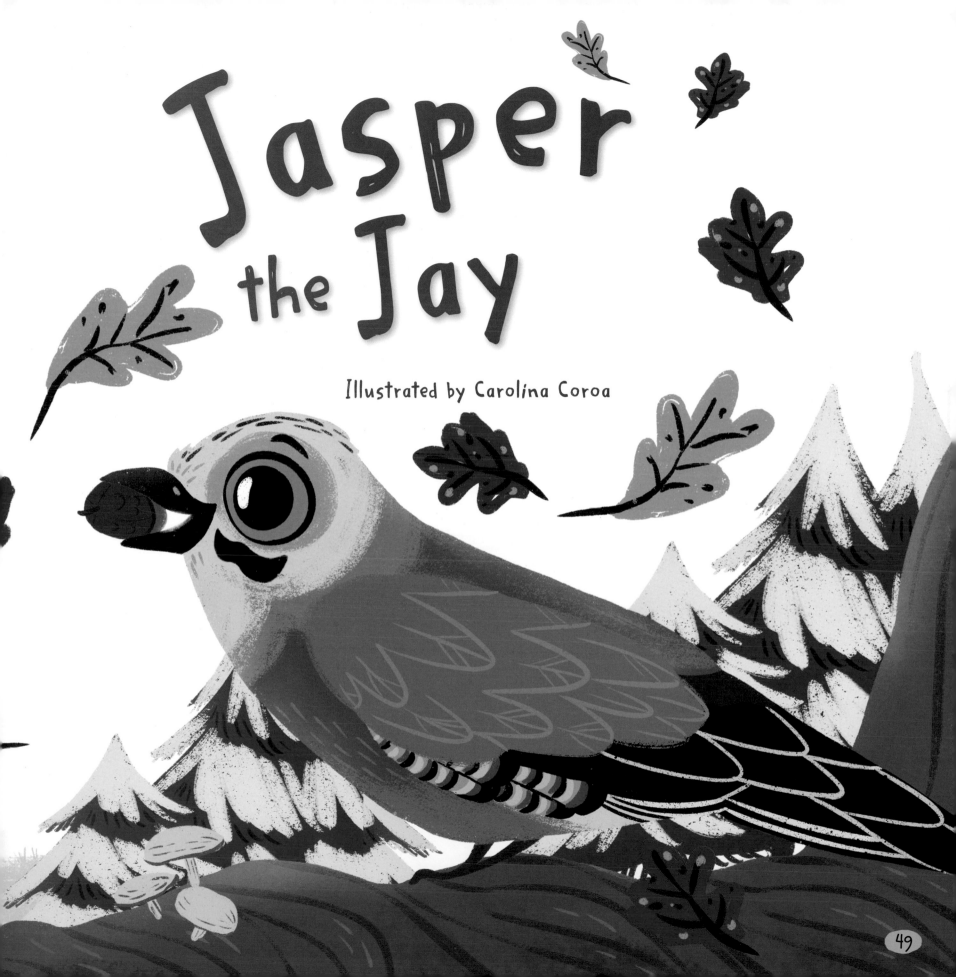

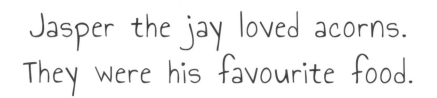

Jasper the jay loved acorns.
They were his favourite food.

Every year in autumn, acorns fell
from oak trees, and Jasper started
collecting and hiding them. He hid
hundreds of acorns in secret
places all over the wood.

When winter came, and
everything was frozen, there
were fewer insects, fruit and
seeds to eat. Many animals
were very hungry.

Jasper was never hungry – he always had more than enough acorns hidden away. But although he had more food than he needed, he would not share it with other animals.

Every day, Jasper flew to each of his hiding places in the wood to check on his acorns. But one morning, something changed.

Jasper met an old jay called Jonas.

"Can I have one of your acorns?" he asked.

No, go away!

Greedy Jasper did not want to share a single acorn.

When Jasper was sure Jonas had
gone, he scraped away the snow at
the bottom of the tree.

"It's gone!" he cried. One of
Jasper's acorns was missing!

The next day, Jasper flew
off to check his acorns. He landed in a
tree that was one of his favourite hiding
places. A woodpecker, whose name was
Walden, was clinging to the trunk.

"Please can I have one of your tasty
acorns?" Walden asked.

"No, I need them all!" replied Jasper.

Walden flew off to search for food elsewhere.

But when Jasper checked inside the hidey-hole in the tree, what did he find?

Noooo! Another acorn has gone!

Jasper had a bad feeling about his acorn stores. On the third morning he met Rae the red squirrel. Rae also asked Jasper for an acorn.

I don't have enough for myself!

When Rae had scampered away,
Jasper looked under the log
she had been sitting on.

Another
one gone!

Jasper was not surprised that
the acorn he had stashed there
was gone. There must be a
thief in the forest!

Jasper set off to find the thief. First he went back to the big beech tree and found Jonas. He was having a nap and dreaming of acorns.

"Have you stolen my acorns?"
asked Jasper.

"Mmmm, acorns..." mumbled Jonas.

Then he opened his eyes
and saw Jasper's cross face.

"I would never steal," he replied.

Jasper flew off in search of Walden the woodpecker.

Tap! Tap! Tap!

Tap! Tap, tap, tappity-tap!

Jasper could hear Walden hammering the trunk with his beak before he saw him.

Walden did not hear Jasper's squawks at first.

"Did you steal my acorns?" shouted Jasper.

Hey! Can you hear me?

Walden stopped hammering.

"Why are you shouting?" he asked. "Of course I didn't steal your acorns."

Jasper set off to look for Rae. He spotted the red squirrel leaping nimbly down a trunk and hovered in her path. But Rae didn't pause, and pushed straight past Jasper.

Hey, mind where you're going!

At Jasper's angry caw,
Rae skidded to a halt.

Did YOU steal my acorns?

Who? Me?

Rae glanced a little nervously over Jasper's shoulder. "Of course not," she said.

None of the animals Jasper questioned owned up to stealing his acorns, so he made a plan to catch the thief.

He chose three of his biggest, tastiest acorns. Then he carefully scratched little crosses on them with his beak.

His busy morning had made
Jasper feel rather sleepy,
and he soon dozed off.

Suddenly he was jolted out of
his nap. Something had fallen
on his head! It was one
of his acorns!

Smack!

Jasper flew up at once to catch the culprit, and there was Rae! She was picking up the other acorns she had dropped.

69

"Um... these acorns are mine," said Rae.

But when Jasper showed her the scratches on the acorns, Rae knew she was caught!

I am sorry, but I was so hungry.

Then Jasper felt sorry for being so mean.

"In winter there is less food in the forest, so I will share my acorns with all of you in future," he said.

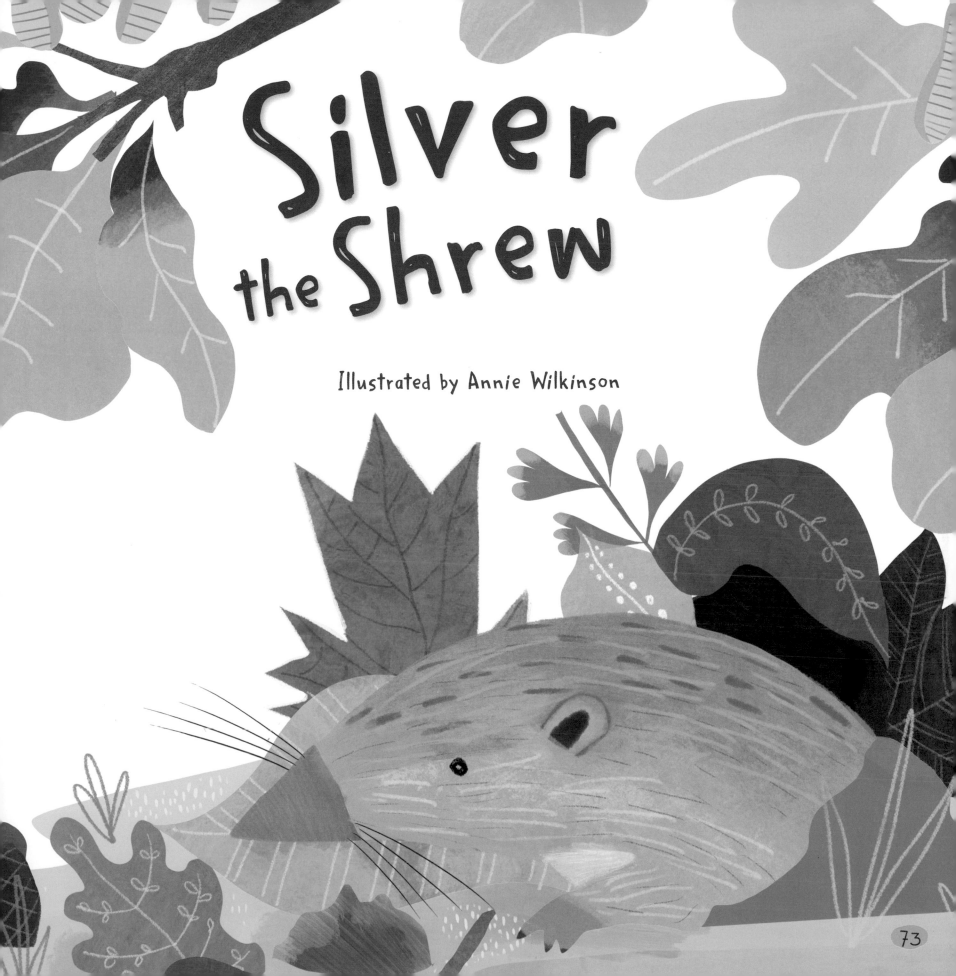

Silver
the Shrew

Illustrated by Annie Wilkinson

Autumn was the time when many young animals left their homes, and the woodland was full of nuts, berries and fungi. Animals were fattening up or storing food for winter, when there was less to eat.

Silver the shrew lived in a nest with his brothers and sisters. Soon they would all leave home, but first Silver wanted to get up to some mischief.

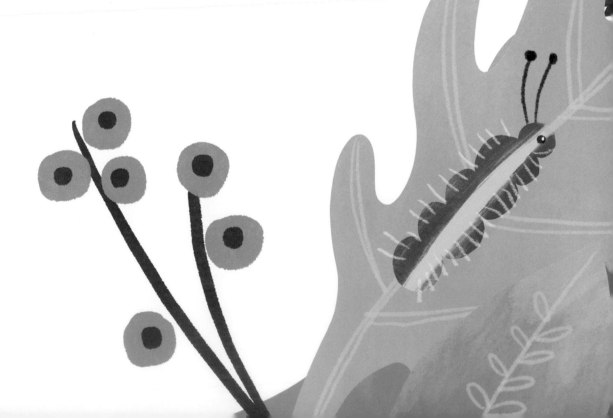

Zzzzz

Silver was always getting up to mischief.
This particular morning, when he was
supposed to be napping with his family,
he crept outside in search of an acorn.

Silver pushed the acorn hard into the nest and **SMACK!** All the young shrews woke up.

"What was that?" said Silver's little sister.

"Danger!" shouted their mother.
"We must move nests!"

Naughty Silver did not tell them about the acorn.
So all of the young shrews followed their mother out
into the cool morning, holding on to each other's tails.

"Stay close to me," said mother shrew.

Soon they met a prickly hedgehog, whose name
was Hettie. She had been hunting for juicy worms
and slugs all night, so was looking for a
cosy place to curl up and sleep.

"Hurry up Silver!" called his mother. Silver was dragging his paws as he was looking for something naughty to do next.

SPLAT! A blackberry exploded everywhere.

"Eww!" cried Silver's sister, as Silver giggled beside her.

SPLAT!

"What have you done?" asked mother shrew. "You are so naughty Silver!" She hurried them away before they woke the dormouse, to whom the blackberries belonged.

Up ahead, Silver spotted a red squirrel. She was burying something and kept looking around to see if anyone was watching. When she spotted the shrews she darted up a tree.

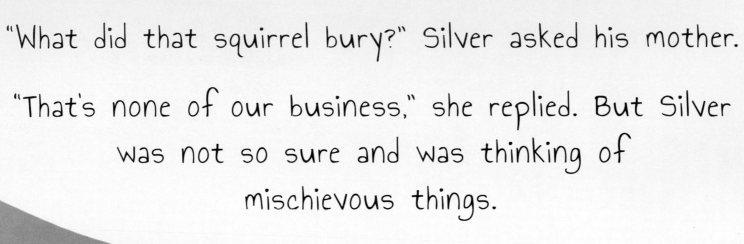

"What did that squirrel bury?" Silver asked his mother.

"That's none of our business," she replied. But Silver was not so sure and was thinking of mischievous things.

It felt like they had been
walking forever.

"How far is our new home?"
asked one of Silver's brothers.

"It's just past that tree with
the twirling seeds," said
mother shrew.

But Silver was not listening, as he was thinking of what mischief he could get up to next. He let go of his sister's tail and slipped away.

Silver headed back to where he had spotted the secretive squirrel. He scraped away the leaves to find... an acorn!

"Is that all?" Silver laughed. Shrews did not eat acorns. But Silver still thought it would be funny to dig up all the squirrel's acorns and hide them.

Hiding the squirrel's acorns gave
Silver an idea of the next naughty
thing he could do. He made his
way back to the home of the
dormouse, whose name
was Denis.

All of the blackberries and hazelnuts were
still there, as Denis was fast asleep. One at
a time, Silver quietly piled Denis' treats on
a leaf and then dragged them away.

It did not take Silver long to find the next animal to play a joke on. He heard Hettie's spikes rustling in the leaves.

"Excuse me," Silver said bravely.

"Please tell me where it is," said Hettie.

Silver sent Hettie towards the stream. But do you think he had really seen a cosy spot for her?

I've seen a cosy spot for you to sleep.

Silver had caused a lot of trouble this time!
He ran through the wood. Not far behind
him was a furious Hettie.

Come
back here!

Hey!

She was followed by an angry Denis.

"Where have you hidden my blackberries and hazelnuts?" he cried. Then Denis was followed by a furious red squirrel, named Sylvie.

Stop, you naughty shrew!

Silver reached his new nest,
and dived in. Where were his
brothers and sisters?

"They have left home," said Silver's mother. "You will stay with me until you can learn to respect other animals."

Silver realized it was time to stop being naughty. He wanted to prove that he could be good, and he said sorry to all the animals he had upset. Just a week later, he left home.

Bye Mum!